STAR WARS™

R2-D2
THE BRAVE

First published in Great Britain 2017 by Egmont UK Limited
The Yellow Building, 1 Nicholas Road, London W11 4AN

ISBN 978 1 4052 8496 7
65568/1

Printed in EU.

Utinni! Droids for Sale!, *Wampa War*, *The Skywalker Collection*, *The Missing Millennium Falcon*, *The Endor Incident and The* Falcon *Awakens* written by Ace Landers.

Item name: LEGO® Star Wars. 2-IN-1 FLIP OVER READER:
R2-D2 THE BRAVE/HAN SOLO'S ADVENTURES
Series: LNR
Item number: LNR-305/306
Batch: 01/GB

 Produced by AMEET Sp. z o.o.
under license from the LEGO Group.

AMEET Sp. z o.o.
Nowe Sady 6, 94-102 Łódź - Poland
ameet@ameet.pl
www.ameet.pl

Distributed by Egmont UK Limited.

Please keep the Egmont UK Limited address for future reference.

www.LEGO.com
www.starwars.co.uk

R2-D2 THE BRAVE

CONTENTS

WHAT YOU SHOULD KNOW ABOUT R2-D2

The Brave Astromech

You've probably heard of R2-D2, the bravest droid in the galaxy. He's the one who looks a bit like an old washing machine. But don't be fooled by his looks – R2 is a skilled starship mechanic and a fighter pilot's assistant. This resourceful little droid has served many masters, from senators to princesses, and even Jedi Knights. But you're more likely to see him in the company of the talkative, golden protocol droid C-3PO. Wherever R2-D2 goes, C-3PO (often reluctantly) follows. The two inseparable droids have been on many adventures together, bravely rescuing their friends and masters from peril.

WHAT YOU SHOULD KNOW ABOUT R2-D2

The Mission

During the hardest days of the Rebel Alliance's struggle with the Empire, only the most trusted spies could carry out the really dangerous missions. When Princess Leia's secret mission was endangered, she could count on her most reliable droid — R2-D2. She hid the stolen plans of a huge Imperial battle station called the Death Star inside the droid, and sent him to deliver them to an old Jedi Master named Obi-Wan Kenobi. The faithful droid set off on the dangerous mission. Not alone of course — C-3PO went along, but he wasn't all that happy about it. On this mission, the greatest adventure in the galaxy began, and the following stories tell only small bits of the adventures that were to come …

UTINNI! DROIDS FOR SALE!

The twin suns of Tatooine were bright in the sky as two rebel droids, R2-D2 and C-3PO, wandered into the hot, sandy hills.

"Well, this is another fine mess you've gotten us into, Artoo," said C-3PO. The droid looked up into the sky. "Surely Princess Leia is worried about us. Let's wait for her to come back."

R2-D2 twirled his head in disagreement. *Whirr Wheet Bling Bloop.*

"Oh you and your Obi-Wan Kenobi," said C-3PO. "You've got sand in your gears if you think we're going to find anyone in the middle of this desert. The chances of being found out here are 725 to ... WHOA!"

C-3PO jumped out of the way as a large, brown transport vehicle stormed over the dune and almost crashed into the droids.

"Well, I've been wrong before," said C-3PO.

A giant door opened at the front of the vehicle and a group of small creatures wearing full-length robes stepped out.

"Hello, children," C-3PO said to the creatures. "Are your parents inside? We need a ride to the nearest —"

But before C-3PO could finish his sentence, the creatures yelled, "Utinni!" and zapped the droids with an electric shock from their ion blasters.

When C-3PO and R2-D2 came to, they were in a strange, rumbling room filled with broken droids. "Artoo, I don't think we're on the consular ship anymore," C-3PO sighed.

R2-D2 whistled and motioned to the other droids that were cobbled together from spare parts.

"Oh dear, you are right, Artoo," said C-3PO. "We've been trapped by Jawas! What *are* they going to do to us? I really don't want to end up like ... them."

A WED droid waved hello with all its arms. Next to it, a malfunctioning medical droid grabbed an unwilling Jawa and busily wrapped him up like a tiny mummy. The Jawa zapped the droid and walked away, leaving bandages piled up on the ground.

"Well, stealing droids is one thing, but being a litter bug is unacceptable." C-3PO picked up the bandages and went to throw them away in a rubbish bin, but the bin started to waddle angrily after C-3PO.

"I'm terribly sorry," said C-3PO as he ran from the bin. R2-D2 broke between them with a *Bleep Birp We-Ow!* The rubbish bin let out a flat *Buzz Buzz* and waddled away.

"Why didn't you tell me the rubbish bin was a Gonk droid?" complained C-3PO.

Whirrrr, scolded R2-D2 as the Jawa Sandcrawler finally stopped and the large doors opened. Jawas ushered the droids out into a bustling city of landspeeders, starships and buildings.

"Welcome to Mos Eisley," yelled a grumpy, ugly man. "I need some help over at the cantina, but I don't know much about droids. Which ones are good?"

The Jawas shoved C-3PO and R2-D2 front and centre first, followed by the WED, Gonk and medical droids.

But then two stormtroopers interrupted the sale and pointed at C-3PO and R2-D2. "We are looking for a pair of droids that look exactly like those two."

The Jawas shook their heads, waved their arms and screeched.

"What?" asked one of the stormtroopers.

"They said *move along,*" said the cantina owner. "These droids belong to the cantina."

"Hey, that's our line!" said the head stormtrooper. He looked over the strange collection of droids. "Yuck. These can't be the droids we're looking for. They look like space junk. Move along."

"OK," said the cantina owner. "Droids, follow me. We'll see if you'll do."

Inside the cantina was dark and filled with tables of mean-looking customers. A jukebox in the corner was playing loud music. Everyone kept to themselves.

"You, with all the arms, you're the chef," the cantina owner told the WED droid.

The WED droid rolled into the kitchen and expertly picked up a set of spatulas, put on a chef's hat then started cooking up a storm.

"Hmmm, I think this is going to work out just fine," the man said. Then he turned to C-3PO. "How about you, Goldie, what can you do?"

"I can speak over six million languages," boasted C-3PO. "In fact —"

"Fine," interrupted the man. "Take this burger with onion rings to the customer at table five. Move it! As for you, little tin cans ..."

"That seems like an easy job," said C-3PO, as the owner lost interest in him and started assigning tasks to R2-D2 and the other droids. He flexed the gears in his arms, picked up the first order, a hamburger with onion rings, and carried it over to a dark booth in the back of the room where a young man and a large Wookiee sat.

"Here's your order, sir," said C-3PO.

"About time. I flew the Kessel Run faster than it took you to deliver my food," snapped the customer at table five. "Wait a minute,

I didn't order onion rings. Everyone knows Han Solo orders the Han-burger with *Falcon* fries. This must be yours, Chewie."

The furry giant next to Han Solo reached for the plate, but then a green hand snuck in.

"No way! Greedo ordered first!" said the green alien. "Greedo ordered first a long time ago! Now give me that burger!"

C-3PO nodded and tried to hand the plate to Greedo when the furry beast roared.

"Never take a Wookiee's plate away until he's finished," warned Han. But it was too late.

Chewie smacked the plate into the air and the hamburger landed on the Gonk droid. The power droid instantly fried the burger until it burnt. Chewie began to howl with anger.

Meanwhile, some of the other customers in the cantina were pressing buttons on R2-D2.

"What's wrong with this jukebox?" asked one of them. "It doesn't play any music."

"Hey, Goldie, your jukebox friend is a dud," called the owner, as he pushed the medical droid forwards. "You, take over for Goldie. And Goldie, you get on stage and sing."

"I am not programmed to sing," said C-3PO. "But whatever you want, boss. Show them what you're capable of, Artoo! Drop a funky beat!"

Rolling up onto the stage, R2-D2 let out a bass-thumping groove while C-3PO joined him. "Well ... my name is C-to-the-3PO, I'm chill as ... erm ... ice on Tatooine. On the run from Darth Vader, we're looking for some guy,

named Obi-Wan Kenobi ... erm ... Does anybody here know him?"

Everyone in the cantina stopped what they were doing and watched C-3PO's horrible rapping. "Boooo!" they all cried, as they rushed the stage to stop the droids from ever trying to make music again.

"Oh my, you must all know where we can find Obi-Wan!" said C-3PO. But then he tripped off the stage and bumped into Chewie, who dropped his brand-new hamburger on the floor.

Chewie roared and pushed C-3PO into the crowd. Suddenly everyone was shoving each other as the dance floor grew wild.

"Wait, wait!" cried the cantina owner, whose club was being destroyed. He had to think of something fast to stop this wild dancing. "Free ice cream! On the house!" he shouted.

"Free ice cream," the WED droid repeated. "On the house."

The WED droid moved behind the bar and rapidly hurled globs of ice cream directly into the crowd.

"No, no, no!" cried the owner. "*On the house* means you can have it for free, not *you can throw ice cream all over the house*! Who's going to clean up this sticky mess?"

Meanwhile, the medical droid hurried onto the dance floor, trying to bandage up people who might be hurt.

Dodging the ice cream, R2-D2 rolled into the chaos to save C-3PO. He balanced C-3PO on the top of his dome and raced out of the crowd. "I'm sorry, pardon us, excuse us," C-3PO apologised over and over again.

"That's it!" screamed the owner, firing a blaster into the air. Instantly, the mayhem stopped and the customers went back to their tables.

"You droids are all fired! And from now on, no droids are ever allowed back here!"

"Pardon me, sir, but do you mean ..." started C-3PO, but the Jawas zapped him again before he made any more trouble and ushered the droids back into their transport.

The Jawa Sandcrawler sped into the desert. There was a rumour about a moisture farm in the middle of nowhere inhabited by a farmer and his gullible helper. It would be the perfect place to sell the no-good droids.

Once Owen Lars and Luke Skywalker bought C-3PO and R2-D2, the Jawas zoomed away and cheered "Utinni!", pleased that the meddlesome droids were gone. The cheer was so loud it echoed across the galaxy ... all the way to the Imperial Death Star.

WAMPA WAR

A freezing breeze whipped through the snowy cliffs on the ice planet, Hoth. Luke Skywalker halted his tauntaun, took a deep breath and smiled.

"Ahhhh, isn't it great here, Han?"

"Sure, it's great, kid," replied Han Solo. "If you like being a rebel ice lolly. Tell me again why you chose this planet for our secret base?"

"Because it's nowhere near as hot as Tatooine," said Luke.

"Oh, I thought it was because no one in their right mind would ever come to this uninhabitable ball of ice and snow," said Han under his breath.

"What did you say?" asked Luke. The heavy wind whistled around them.

"I, ummm, said, I don't see any Imperial probe droids out here," said Han.

"Well then, let's keep looking," Luke said cheerfully. "It's a great day outside. Snow as far as the eye can see."

"Aren't you worried about Darth Vader and the Empire finding us after what we did to their newest toy?" asked Han, referring to the Empire's massive weapon, the Death Star, which the rebels had just destroyed.

"It's hard to be worried in this winter wonderland," said Luke, as he guided his tauntaun onwards. Behind him was his trusty droid co-pilot, R2-D2, being pulled on a sledge.

Brrrrrrrrrrrrrrrr, the droid said.

"Even R2-D2 hates these scouting missions, kid," said Han. "I bet he can't feel his motherboard any more."

"I c-c-c-concur, s-s-s-sir," stuttered a nearly frozen C-3PO, who was on a pair of skis riding behind Han's tauntaun. "I'm p-p-p-programmed for warm weather!"

"Listen to Threepio, Luke!" said Han. "For once, his logic makes sense! There's nothing out here! Let's go back to the base and get some soup and hot chocolate."

The young Jedi stopped and spotted a strange, furry beast in the distance. "Wow! Did you see that? It's a rare wampa sighting!"

Luke eased his tauntaun forward, but the animal kicked in fear and launched R2-D2's sledge down the snowy hillside.

Whhheeeeeeee! screeched R2-D2.

"Ugh, that droid always runs away!" said Luke.

"Doesn't he know that we've already found Obi-Wan Kenobi?" asked C-3PO.

Han sighed. "OK, let's go and get rust-bucket before he gets into real trouble."

"Yay! Maybe we'll spot another wampa!" said Luke.

"C'mon, kid, we're not talking about Wookiees here," warned Han. "If we see a wampa, run away."

The rebels raced after the droid as he slid over the ice.

"That's the fastest I've ever seen Artoo move!" said Han. "If I didn't know any better, I'd say he was enjoying this!"

When they finally caught up with R2-D2, the droid had fallen off the sledge and was rolling around in the snow.

"What a great idea!" said Luke. He jumped off his tauntaun, laid down in the snow and moved his arms and legs back and forth.

"What are you doing?" asked Han.

"Making snow angels," said Luke. "They are way better than the sand angels I used to make on Tatooine. And ... hey, what are those?"

The young Jedi pointed to a collection of large footprints all around them in the snow.

"These definitely aren't from a probe droid," said Han.

"I have a b-b-b-bad f-f-f-feeling about this," said C-3PO as the heroes' tauntauns quickly fled the scene.

Slowly, out of a set of caves that surrounded the rebels, a group of wampas appeared.

Uh-oh, beeped R2-D2. They were surrounded. The first wampa picked up the droid and studied it.

"Hey, you walking carpets," called out Han Solo. "Trust me, I want to deprogramme him

just as much as you do, but you'd better let our friend go."

"That's right! Hands off our buddy, you abominable snowmen!" hollered Luke, as he drew his lightsaber and waved it at the creatures.

The wampa looked confused, but then R2-D2 gave it a shock. The beast drop-kicked the droid like a hockey puck and let out a horrible howl as R2 zipped away through the frozen countryside.

"I warned you," said Han. "That droid is a handful."

The wampas retreated into their caves and for a moment it seemed like the problem was solved.

"OK, let's go and find your soon-to-be-scrap-pile of a droid," said Han.

"Wait, I think we misunderstood the wampas," suggested Luke. "They're coming back with food for us."

The wampas walked out of their caves holding bizarre-looking frozen vegetables like weapons.

"That's not for us, kid," yelled Han. "That's a side dish ... and *we're* the main course!"

The wampas suddenly charged and swung their veggies at Luke, but the Jedi easily sliced and diced their clubs into tiny pieces.

Another set of wampas ran towards them. Han fired a few warning shots to scatter the beasts, but they shielded themselves with pots and pans. The blast ricocheted until it struck a set of sticks underneath a giant pot the size of a bathtub and started a fire.

Then a wampa knocked Han's blaster into the boiling pot. And another wampa knocked Luke's lightsaber into the pot as well.

"Hey! That lightsaber was a collector's item!" whined Luke.

But the wampas hollered back. The rebels were totally trapped.

"I will save you, Master Luke!" cried C-3PO as he tried to ski into the wampas, but the droid slammed into the monsters and burst apart. "Oh dear. I've heard of falling apart in high pressure situations, but this is ridiculous," he added.

"OK, guys, the food fight is over," said Han. "I don't suppose we could offer you some grub from the cafeteria at the secret base instead?"

The wampas grabbed Han and Luke and strung them up over the giant pot filled with boiling water.

"Hey, something smells good," admitted Luke. They both looked down into the pot and noticed all the sliced, diced and blasted veggies floating in a soupy broth. "OK, now *I* really hate scouting missions."

"Why do so many creatures in this galaxy want to eat us?" asked Han.

But before Luke could venture an answer, a rumbling sound came from outside the cave. It was giant snowball. All of the wampas quickly scattered at the sight.

"I never thought I'd be happy to see an avalanche," said Han.

"That's not an avalanche," corrected Luke. "That's Artoo!"

On top of the tumbling snowball was R2-D2, guiding it right into the wampas like an oversized

bowling ball. The creatures tried to run, but the droid rolled over them one by one.

Then R2-D2 launched a grappling hook and pulled Luke and Han to safety. Han jumped up and started collecting C-3PO's parts. Luke jumped up, fished out their weapons from the pot and gave the soup a taste test.

"Yum!" said Luke. "These wampas sure know how to cook! I've never thought of using my lightsaber in the kitchen. It really gives the veggies a smoky flavour."

"Not now, Chef Skywalker! Help me pick up Threepio and let's get out of here!" Han called out. "There are more wampas on the way and they look hungry!"

The rebels ran for their tauntauns, but the wampa herd was fast.

"Wait!" called out Luke. "Where's Artoo?"

"I'm afraid it's every droid for themselves now!" said C-3PO.

As the herd grew closer, something sped by the rebels. It was R2-D2 with his rocket blasters! He was dragging a large empty pot behind him. Han and Luke tossed C-3PO's parts into the pot and quickly jumped inside it.

"Hold on, everybody!" screamed Han. "We're going wampa bowling!"

R2-D2 slung the pot around like a yo-yo and the heroes knocked down every wampa in sight.

Brrreeep Boop Wheee-urp, said R2-D2, as the dizzy rebels climbed out into the snow.

"Easy for you to say," said Han.

"Can we go on the ride again? Can we go on the ride again? Please!" begged Luke, jumping up and down with excitement.

C-3PO called out from inside the pot. "Can someone give me a hand? I mean, literally, I cannot find my hand in here."

"OK, everybody," said Han, passing C-3PO his hand. "That's enough adventure for today. Let's head back to the base where it's safe."

Suddenly thunderous footsteps boomed in the distance. The rebels turned to watch a squadron of Empire AT-ATs walking towards their secret base.

"Han, look!" cheered Luke. "Can I have one of those, please?"

"It's a wonder you're still alive," said Han. "Now let's go and save the base before those overgrown dog-walkers crush my precious *Millennium Falcon*!"

THE SKYWALKER COLLECTION

With Han Solo trapped in carbonite and missing, it was up to the rebels to try to find him.

"To find Han we'll need to think like Boba Fett," said Princess Leia. "Who could think like a no-good, double-crossing traitor?"

Everyone aboard the rebel ship *Redemption* looked at Lando Calrissian.

"One time I hand you over to Darth Vader," cried Lando. "One time! Now suddenly I'm one of the worst people in the entire galaxy?"

"Yes," answered everyone in the room.

Lando gave them a cool, charming smile. "But at least I looked *good* being *bad*, right?"

"No," answered everyone in the room.

"OK, OK," said Lando. "It doesn't take a genius to guess that Boba Fett is taking Han to Jabba the Hutt on Tatooine."

So Leia led a rebel crew to rescue Han, leaving C-3PO and R2-D2 to keep watch over Luke while he rested from his battle with Darth Vader.

But little did the rebels know that Boba Fett had been sent on a second mission by the Emperor to collect Luke Skywalker.

"That's right," the Emperor told Boba Fett. "I simply must complete my Skywalker collection!"

Aboard the Death Star II, Darth Vader and Boba Fett admired the Emperor's prize room.

"But Emperor," said Darth Vader, "I can bring Skywalker to you."

"Bah, Vader!" exclaimed the Emperor. "You've had your chance, and three times you've let that kid slip past you. Let's give someone else a turn. So what's your plan, Fett?"

Boba pulled on a hooded cape. He still looked suspicious.

"The rebels will still see you coming!" complained Darth Vader. "I have a cape, the Emperor has a hooded cloak. It's the most evil attire in the galaxy."

But then Boba Fett held up the most devious weapon in the world: a rebel visitor pass.

"Hmmm, Vader, maybe you're going to get your next shot after all," grumbled the Emperor, who didn't believe in the power of the visitor pass. But then Boba Fett held it up and alarm sensors all around the Death Star went off.

"Rebel intruder! Rebel intruder!"

As soon as he put it back under his cloak, the alarm stopped.

"Oh, wow," the Emperor said with excitement. "I can't believe that actually worked."

So while the other heroes were searching for Boba Fett, the bounty hunter himself snuck into the rebel ship to kidnap Luke.

Hiding behind the rebel visitor pass, Boba Fett strolled into the main hub of the rebel ship *Redemption*. He was surrounded by rebel soldiers, but no one noticed him. This mission was going to be easier than he thought.

But then the red-skinned Admiral Ackbar walked by.

"Hey! You!" he called out, putting his arm around Boba Fett. "There are two things I always know how to spot — a trap and a friendly visitor who needs a guided tour. Now, come with me, ummmm," he paused to read Boba Fett's pass, "Luke! We have a Jedi named Luke aboard this ship, too! Would you like to meet him?"

Boba Fett nodded in agreement.

"Attaboy," cheered Ackbar, as he led the bounty hunter right to his target.

"Say, you look a bit familiar. Have we met before?"

Boba Fett shook his head.

"Hmmmm, it must be your evil-looking cape. But I see you have a rebel visitor pass, so you must be trustworthy." Ackbar let out a hearty laugh. "Here we are. Behind this door is the great Luke Skywalker. He destroyed the Death Star, fought Darth Vader and lived to tell the tale!"

As the door slid open, Boba Fett spotted Luke and unholstered his blaster. But before the bounty hunter could do any damage, R2-D2 jumped into action and moved Luke's bed behind a curtain. Boba took one step forward, but was stopped by C-3PO.

"I am quite sorry," the droid apologised. "Master Luke is not signing autographs at the moment due to a … um … hand cramp.

But if you really want an autograph, the line starts over there."

Boba turned to see a long line of rebel fans waiting for the Jedi.

"But Threepio, it's me, Admiral Ackbar," said Boba's new tour guide. "Can't you spare Luke for one quick hello?"

"Sorry, Admiral," said C-3PO. "No exceptions."

The door whooshed shut in Boba Fett's face.

"Come on, there's so much more to see!" cheered Ackbar, as he pulled Boba away to continue their tour.

Back inside Luke's room, R2-D2 had not been fooled by the fake visitor pass. He knew that Boba Fett was up to no good. *Bleep! Beep! Bop!*

"Boba Fett?" repeated C-3PO. "Here on a rebel ship? That's impossible, Artoo. You must have picked up a bug on Dagobah. That was just a visitor named Luke. Didn't you read his pass?"

R2-D2 made a frustrated whirring noise and moved Luke into the last place that Boba Fett would look for him: a sauna. Draped in towels, the droids

relaxed as they hid in clouds of steam while Luke slept.

"And here's the place that most rebels love!" cried Admiral Ackbar, as he burst into the sauna with his mysterious visitor. "Phew! But not me. It's *way* too hot in here."

Quickly, R2-D2 warned C-3PO a second time and pushed Luke's bed away, turning up the heat in the room as they escaped. Steam and smoke erupted everywhere. Fett tried to follow

Skywalker, but his mask fogged up. Then Ackbar grabbed his arm and ushered him back into the hallway.

"Let's get out of here before we both get cooked," said the admiral.

When Boba Fett emerged from the room, his cape had shrunk down three sizes and barely

covered him. So before Ackbar recognised him, Boba Fett pointed towards the nearest door, as if to enquire about what was inside.

"Oh, this is an exciting room, because it's the ..." *WHAM!* Fett didn't wait for his guide to finish. He shoved Ackbar inside, slammed the door shut and locked it.

Meanwhile, R2-D2 finally convinced C-3PO that Boba Fett was on board the rebel ship by showing him a picture from the ship's cameras of Fett pushing Ackbar into a closet.

"Well, I'll be a wampa's Wookiee!" exclaimed C-3PO. "It's that no good bounty hunter! We need to hide Master Luke! That ship looks safe."

C-3PO took hold of Luke's bed and pushed him aboard the *Slave I*, Boba Fett's own ship.

As C-3PO came back outside, R2-D2 went berserk with beeps and blorps, but before C-3PO realised his mistake, Boba Fett darted past the droids and onto his ship with Luke Skywalker as his prisoner.

"That did not go quite as I'd planned," admitted C-3PO.

R2-D2 nudged C-3PO into an X-wing. They were the only ones who could save Luke now!

C-3PO threw the ship directly into hyperdrive. But Boba Fett hadn't even left the ship's bay. When the droids finally stopped, they sat in front of a partially constructed Death Star.

"Oh, that doesn't look good ..." said C-3PO. "I suggest a new strategy, Artoo. *You* drive."

R2-D2 took control and raced back to the *Redemption* only to find *Slave I* was trapped by a set of robotic docking arms controlled by Ackbar. He had been shoved and locked into the docking control booth.

"Wait, friend. I have so much more of the ship to show you!" Ackbar called out over the radio.

"Great work, Admiral," cheered C-3PO. "You caught Boba Fett!"

"I did?" asked Ackbar. "I mean, yes, of course, I did. You're welcome!"

But Fett wasn't finished fighting and he fought dirty. In a last ditch effort to escape, he tried to jettison Luke into space.

Immediately, R2-D2 launched himself out of the X-wing and grabbed his friend who was in a deep slumber. Then the droid used his rockets to safely jet back to the *Redemption*. During all the commotion, Boba Fett gave Ackbar the slip and blasted away into hyperspace.

Back on board the medical ship, Luke finally woke up. "Awww, come on, guys. You let me sleep in? We're never going to find Boba Fett if we just lie around this boring old ship all day!"

GLOSSARY

ADMIRAL ACKBAR

Admiral Gial Ackbar commands the rebel starfleet. He led the rebel assault on the second Death Star from his flagship *Home One*. His favourite starship is *Daisy Mae*, his own Delta 7B Aethersprite-class light interceptor.

ALDERAAN

A peaceful planet where Princess Leia grew up. Known as a world that supported rebel activity, Alderaan was destroyed by the Empire's first Death Star.

ASTROMECH DROID

Special droids that help with navigation and repairing starships.

AT-AT

A four-legged, walking transport and combat vehicle used by the Imperial ground forces. It is over 20 metres tall and is heavily armed and armoured.

BB-8

A small astromech droid that accompanied Poe Dameron, the best pilot of the Resistance, on many missions – including the one on Jakku where they obtained a vital clue to the location of the missing Luke Skywalker.

BLASTER

An energy weapon that is popular in the galaxy. It fires bolts that look like laser beams.

BOBA FETT

Son of bounty hunter, Jango Fett. Boba also becomes a famous bounty hunter over the years. He flies *Slave I*, a heavily-armed starship that he inherited from his father.

BOUNTY HUNTER

Someone who tracks and captures wanted persons for payment.

CARBONITE

A liquid substance made from carbon gas that can become solid through rapid freezing. On Vader's order, Han Solo was frozen in it and given to Boba Fett, who took him to Jabba the Hutt.

C-3PO
A golden protocol droid, who often acts as a translator. He was built by Anakin Skywalker and later serves his son, Luke. He is commonly seen alongside his counterpart, R2-D2.

CANTINA
The Mos Eisley cantina on Tatooine is a dimly-lit tavern, known to be a place visited by most star pilots, smugglers and all kinds of shady characters.

CHEWBACCA
Loyal friend of smuggler-turned-rebel, Han Solo. The Wookiee is his co-pilot aboard the *Millennium Falcon*.

DAGOBAH
A distant, swamp-covered planet strong with the Force. This is where Luke Skywalker had his Jedi training from old Jedi Master Yoda.

DARK LORD
Honorary title of evil Sith, like Darth Vader.

DARK SIDE
The side of the Force that is used for evil deeds. The Sith embrace the dark side of the Force.

DARTH VADER
Apprentice of Darth Sidious, aka the evil Emperor Palpatine. At his master's side he spreads fear and loathing in the Empire. He was once the Jedi Anakin Skywalker.

DEATH STAR
A huge battle station in space that looks like a little moon. Its superlaser can destroy whole planets. The first Death Star was destroyed by Luke Skywalker, but the Empire built the Death Star II soon after.

DROIDS
Robots built for various purposes in the galaxy.

EMPEROR
Title of the ruler over the Galactic Empire.

EMPIRE
Association of worlds from all over the galaxy that are ruled by self-proclaimed Emperor Palpatine. The Empire rules by fear and violence.

ENDOR

A small forest moon in a remote corner of the galaxy, where the Empire built a shield generator to protect the incomplete second Death Star. The clash between the rebel and Imperial fleets near Endor led to the fall of the Empire.

EWOK

These small furry creatures live on Endor. They helped the rebels destroy the Imperial outpost, which allowed the destruction of the second Death Star.

FINN

A young man trained from birth to serve the First Order as a stormtrooper (designated FN-2187). Shocked by the First Order's cruelty, he deserted and joined the resistance.

THE FORCE

An invisible energy that flows through everything and binds the galaxy together. Jedi and Sith can feel and use it – for good deeds, as well as for evil ones.

GALAXY

Conglomerate of billions of star systems with countless planets.

GONK DROID

The GNK power droids are nothing more than big, walking batteries. They are often called "Gonk" droids due to the sounds they make.

GREEDO

A Rodian bounty hunter working for Jabba the Hutt.

HAN SOLO

A smuggler who joins the Rebel Alliance. Together with his friend Chewbacca, he flies the *Millennium Falcon*.

HOTH

The sixth planet in the remote system of the same name. This world of snow and ice was the location of the Rebel Alliance's Echo Base.

HYPERDRIVE

A vital part of the starship engine system that allows the vessels to jump into hyperspace and travel faster than the speed of light.

HYPERSPACE

Starships reach hyperspace by flying faster than lightspeed. Through hyperspace they can quickly get from one point of the galaxy to another.

JABBA THE HUTT
One of the galaxy's most powerful gangsters, to whom Han Solo owes a substantial debt. Jabba resides in his palace on Tatooine.

JAWA
The little Jawas live as scavengers in the deserts of Tatooine. They are wily traders and wear dark hooded robes that only show their glowing eyes.

JEDI
Group of followers of the light side of the Force. The Jedi fight for good and are considered to be keepers of peace and justice in the Republic. In the days of the Empire there are only a few of them left.

KESSEL RUN
A hyperspace route used by smugglers to transport spice from the spice mines of Kessel. Han Solo claims to be the one who flew the route the fastest in his *Millennium Falcon*.

LANDO CALRISSIAN
An old friend of Han Solo, Lando was once a smuggler, too. When he was the governor of the Cloud City he betrayed Han to Darth Vader, but later he made up for his mistake and joined the rebels.

LEIA ORGANA
Princess Leia is one of the Rebel Alliance's leaders. Her homeworld, Alderaan, was destroyed by the first Death Star.

LIGHTSABER
A sword with a glowing blade of pure energy that penetrates almost anything. In most cases, Jedi lightsabers have green or blue blades, while Sith lightsabers have red ones.

LUKE SKYWALKER
Hero of the Rebel Alliance who destroyed the first Death Star in his X-wing starfighter. Being Anakin Skywalker's son, he is very strong in the Force and becomes a powerful Jedi.

MILLENNIUM FALCON
An old, patched-up space freighter and – according to its owner, Han Solo – the fastest ship in the galaxy.

MOS EISLEY
City on the desert world Tatooine, with a large spaceport.

OBI-WAN KENOBI

A Jedi Master who fought in the Clone Wars. He trained Anakin Skywalker to become a Jedi, and his son Luke, many years later.

OWEN LARS

A moisture farmer from Tatooine. He and his wife Beru raised their nephew, Luke Skywalker.

PROBE DROID

Imperial probe droids, known as 'probots', were designed for deep space exploration and reconnaissance.

R2-D2

Brave R2-D2, called 'Artoo' by friends, is an astromech droid that helps with navigation and repairing starships. He undergoes many adventures alongside galactic heroes – often together with his counterpart, C-3PO.

REBEL ALLIANCE

Resistance fighters who want to restore a democratic Republic.

REDEMPTION

A massive starship serving in the Rebel Alliance's starfleet as a medical frigate.

REMOTE

A training remote is a miniature spherical droid used by Jedi learners to practise avoiding blaster bolts and deflecting them with lightsabers.

RESISTANCE

Small, secretive military force founded by Leia Organa to combat the First Order, a military and political organisation following the footsteps of the evil Galactic Empire.

REY

A young scavenger girl who grew up on Jakku. Together with Finn, she helped BB-8 get to the headquarters of the Resistance, and discovered her potential in using the Force along the way.

SANDCRAWLER

A huge treaded fortress used by Jawas as shelter and transport.

SITH

Evil Force users who have embraced the dark side and want more and more power. They are arch-enemies of the Jedi. For hundreds of years there have only been two of them at a time – a master and an apprentice.

SLAVE I

A heavily armed starship that belongs to the bounty hunter Boba Fett. He inherited it from his father, Jango Fett.

STORMTROOPERS

The soldiers of the Empire. Stormtroopers wear white armour with a closed helmet, so their faces can't be seen and they all look the same.

TAKODANA

A lush, green world in the galaxy's Western Reaches. Home of Maz Kanata's castle, an open port for travellers of dubious reputation.

TATOOINE

A remote rim world with a mostly desert surface. Besides the native Tusken Raiders and Jawas, there are also settlers from other planets. Jabba the Hutt has his palace here. A popular sport on the planet is podracing.

TAUNTAUN

A species of snow lizard living on Hoth. Rebel troopers from Echo Base rode them during patrol missions on the snow plains of Hoth.

TUSKEN RAIDER

Fearsome inhabitants of the desert wasteland of Tatooine who are quick to attack anyone, anytime and for any reason.

WAMPA

Large snow monster from the planet Hoth that walks upright on two legs. Wampas have white fur, two mighty horns, and sharp teeth and claws. They prefer to eat tauntauns, but do not hesitate to eat humans as well.

WED DROID

WED droids have a flat, treaded base, a spindly neck and a cluster of arms tipped with various tools. They serve as utility and repair droids all over the galaxy.

WOOKIEE

Inhabitants of the forest planet Kashyyyk, who live in tree house cities and have fur all over their bodies. They are very close to nature but also technologically gifted.

X-WING

Fast and well-armoured starfighter used by the Rebel Alliance's pilots. Luke Skywalker flew one during the attack on the first Death Star.

STAR WARS

LEGO

HAN SOLO'S ADVENTURES

HAN SOLO'S ADVENTURES

CONTENTS

WHAT YOU SHOULD KNOW ABOUT HAN SOLO

From Smuggler to Hero

Life is full of surprises if you make a living as a galactic smuggler. Han Solo, the captain of the *Millennium Falcon*, knows that all too well. When he and his friend and co-pilot, a Wookiee named Chewbacca, were offered a hefty fee for taking two strangers and their droids to the planet Alderaan, they thought it was easy money. Shortly after, they were rescuing a princess imprisoned in the Death Star, the evil Empire's battle station! Then, chased by the Imperial fleet, they ended up as part of a team of brave rebels fighting for freedom in the galaxy, and helped destroy the dreaded Death Star! What had seemed to be a quick, one-time deal, began Han's greatest adventure that changed his life completely ...

WHAT YOU SHOULD KNOW ABOUT HAN SOLO

Back in Business

Han Solo became one of the greatest leaders of the Rebel Alliance. And whether he wanted them or not, he was in for many adventures! He saved his friend Luke Skywalker from freezing on planet Hoth, escaped from the mouth of a giant space worm and fell in love with Princess Leia. He was even turned into a carbonite statue and put up in Jabba the Hutt's throne room. It was Han who led the attack on an Imperial base on Endor, which resulted in the destruction of the second Death Star. Many years after the fall of the Empire, Han returned to his smuggling business, lost his beloved ship, found it and ... found himself struggling for freedom in the galaxy again! These stories tell a few of his less known adventures ...

THE MISSING
MILLENNIUM FALCON

Inside the dark Mos Eisley cantina, Han Solo had
just agreed to help two strangers named Obi-Wan
Kenobi and Luke Skywalker. They needed a pilot
and he needed money – lots of money – to pay
back the crime lord Jabba the Hutt.

"Just remember, this is a one-time deal," said Han.

"Aw, but Han, I thought we'd become best
friends on this adventure and take down

Darth Vader and the Empire together," Luke whined. "When you get to know me, you'll see how great I am."

"Being too confident is a path to the dark side," Obi-Wan reminded Luke. "If Han has better things to do, then we must let him go his own way."

Han rolled his eyes. "Listen, guys, it's not you, it's me. I'm a rebel, you know."

"But that's who we want to help! The Rebel Alliance!" cheered Luke.

Han sighed and shook his head. "No, laser brain. I'm not *that* kind of rebel."

Obi-Wan put his arm around Luke and pulled the young Jedi aside. "Excuse my friend's excitement. He's spent his whole life on a moisture farm."

"That explains a lot," said Han. "So when do you want to leave on our one and only mission?"

"As soon as possible," said Obi-Wan.

"All right then," said Han. "Chewie, get the *Millennium Falcon* ready. Then you guys meet us in Docking Bay 94 at one o'clock sharp. And make sure you bring the money."

Luke nodded. "Oh, there's one more thing; we have a pair of droids coming with us on the trip, too. Will that be a problem?"

As Chewie left, Han turned back to Luke. "Depends ... are these droids bounty hunters?"

Luke and Obi-Wan burst out laughing.

"Threepio, a bounty hunter! Can you imagine? No, no, no, the worst Threepio could do is bore you with his constant chit-chat. And Artoo barely says a beep," Luke said.

"You promise?" Han was a little suspicious. "I've been, um, popular with all the wrong people lately. I don't want to fly into a trap."

"Jedi's honour," said Obi-Wan as they stood up to prepare for the journey. "We will see you at one o'clock."

"Jedi's honour," Han repeated sarcastically to himself after they were gone. "Fat lot of good that does to someone who doesn't believe in Jedi or the Force." He left and headed back to Docking Bay 94, where he had parked the *Millennium Falcon* the night before.

"Hey, Chewie, we've got to make room for two droids," said Han as he walked into the hangar. But it was empty - his prized ship was gone! Han paced around, holding his hands out to touch

the ship as if it had simply turned itself invisible. But it hadn't. The *Millennium Falcon* was missing!

As Han searched for clues behind a stack of crates, he heard a deep, gravelly voice bellow from the other side of the room. It sent shivers down his back.

"Solo!" It was Jabba the Hutt. And the crime lord wasn't alone.

"Sir, it looks like Solo already left," said Boba Fett. "His pitiful excuse for a ship is gone."

"You're a pitiful excuse," Han whispered to himself while hiding inside a giant empty box of Soapsuds Starship Cleaner. "I've got to find my ship before those Jedi come back here."

Carefully, Han pushed his feet through the bottom of the box, and shuffled backwards towards the rear entrance of the docking bay. He had just made it outside when he bumped into a patrol of stormtroopers.

"Halt, who goes there?" demanded one stormtrooper.

"Beep, boop, beep?" said Han, acting like a droid from inside the box.

This made the stormtroopers curious. "A droid, eh? You're the weirdest droid I've ever seen. What's your name?"

"Ummmm," Han stalled. "I'm ... Threepio?"

The stormtroopers turned to each other, surprised. "Hey! You're one of the droids we're looking for!"

"Awww, blast it, of course I am," complained Han, as he darted into the busy Mos Eisley streets to escape the stormtroopers.

"After him!" they shouted, chasing the odd-looking droid. But Han was fast and smart. He blasted two eyeholes in the box so he could see where he was going, then headed straight towards the Soapsuds Starship Cleaner store. It was crowded with Soapsuds boxes that

looked exactly like him. Han weaved in between the other boxes and knocked them over, spilling slippery soapsuds into the street. The stormtroopers lost their balance and slid into a pile of bubbles. Han jumped out of the box, but slipped on the suds too, which had mixed with the Tatooine sand and made a mudslide.

Nearby, Obi-Wan, Luke and the droids were close to selling Luke's landspeeder to pay for their flight on the *Falcon*.

"This landspeeder is barely used," said Obi-Wan. "It's only made two cross-Tatooine trips since we've owned it."

"I don't know," said the potential buyer. "These look like Tusken Raider scratches."

"Oh, those?" said Obi-Wan with a nod. "Those will come right out with a little elbow grease and some Soapsuds Starship Cleaner ... WHOA!"

A gigantic wave of mud and slimy gunk washed all over their landspeeder. Han Solo landed in the driver's seat. "Oh, hey there, guys. Small city, huh?"

"No sale," said the no-longer-potential buyer as he walked away.

"Han – you dirty, no good, troublemaker! Is your ship ready?" asked Luke.

"Sure, kid," said Han nervously. "I, um, just need to get a few more things for the trip. Like video games, sweets and crisps ... you know, space travel food."

"But we're still on for one o'clock?" asked Obi-Wan.

"You know it, Jedi-dude," said Han. "Oh, and some words of advice, keep those droids away from any stormtroopers. They do not like whichever one is named Threepio."

"Me?" cried out C-3PO. "What did I do to deserve this?"

"Well, good talk, but I really need to go and do all those things I said I was going to do," said Han, as he climbed out of the filthy landspeeder. "And you should really clean this up if you want to sell it."

"Thanks for the advice," Obi-Wan said flatly, but Han ignored him. He needed to save his own ship.

Han found a computer map containing all 362 docking bays in Mos Eisley. "Wow, that's a lot of places to look, but I've got to start somewhere."

In the first bay, he found Boba Fett's ship, *Slave I.* "Nope, this thing looks like a huge waffle maker."

In the second bay, he found an old, dusty podracer with a grey helmet. There was a name written inside. "Anakin ... what sort of

name is Anakin? I bet everyone picked on him growing up."

In the third bay, Han was met by a chipper voice. "Hello, friend," said a red-faced Mon Calamari. "Ackbar's the name, and staying away

from traps is my game. Feast your eyes on the sweetest ride in the galaxy – the *Daisy Mae*."

"Um, thanks, Ackbar, but I'm looking for the *Millennium Falcon* – the actual sweetest ride in the galaxy."

"The *Millennium Falcon*, you say?" asked Ackbar. "Never heard of it."

Han started to argue, then heard the clock strike one. He was late! As he left the *Daisy Mae*'s bay, he bumped into Obi-Wan and Luke again.

"Great, I found you guys," said Han. "Did you sell your mudspeeder, er, landspeeder?"

"Yes, we did," said Obi-Wan. "I can be very convincing. Now where is your ship?"

"Right here," said Han.

As they walked into Docking Bay 94, Han held his breath and prepared his best excuse, but he didn't need to. Miraculously, the *Millennium Falcon* had returned and it was gleaming!

"That's it?" bemoaned Obi-Wan, Luke and C-3PO at the same time.

"That's it!" cheered Han, as Chewie walked down the entry plank. He grabbed the Wookiee and whispered "Chewie! Where have you been? And what happened to the ship?"

Girrrffff, roared Chewie.

"Oh, you took it to get cleaned because we ran out of Soapsuds Starship Cleaner!" said Han. "You scared me, Chewie, but the *Falcon* looks like a million credits now!"

"It looks like a shiny, new waffle maker to me," said Luke.

"But it flies like a dream," said Han. "Now get on board before I change my mind about going on this one-time-only adventure with you."

THE ENDOR INCIDENT

Under the shadows of the forest, Han Solo jumped onto a fallen tree and took a deep breath.

"Wow, is it beautiful out here or what? Say, when do we get to make a campfire and tell ghost stories to scare Threepio?"

C-3PO popped out from behind a tree. His metal knees began to shake and he said nervously:

"G-g-g-ghosts! Did someone say ghosts?"

"Shhhh!" scolded Luke Skywalker, peeking out from his hiding spot behind another tree. "Han, get down before someone sees you. Remember, we're on a mission. And you know we can't joke about ghosts in front of Threepio."

It was true. Han and Luke were part of a secret rebel strike team sent to the forest moon of Endor. The Empire had built a second Death Star that was protected by an energy field generator hidden somewhere in the forest. It was up to Han, Luke, Princess Leia, Chewbacca, C-3PO and R2-D2 to disrupt

the energy field so that the rebels could destroy the new Death Star.

It was also true that poor C-3PO did not like ghost stories.

"Come on, kid, no one is going to find us," said Han, as he gestured towards the empty forest around them. "We're in the middle of nowhere. I could scream at the top of my lungs, 'Hey, Empire, we're the rebels and we want to destroy your Death Star!' and we'd be perfectly fine."

Slowly, the other rebels came out from their hiding spots and joined Han.

"Han has a point, Luke," said Leia. "I haven't seen any sign of stormtroopers in this forest. All this hiding is slowing us down."

The Jedi reluctantly agreed. "OK."

"See, Luke," said Han. "It's just the six of us out here ... and those biker scouts who are watching us from their speeder bikes over there ... Uh-oh!"

The biker scouts paused on their speeders. One of them pulled out a transmitter to call for backup, but Han blasted the comlink out of his hand. The biker scout fell off of his speeder, but caught onto the other trooper as he took off to warn the Empire about the rebels. Instantly, the biker scout was dragged into the forest, leaving his speeder behind.

"Don't worry, everyone, I'll catch them before they reach their base," said Han.

But Luke and Princess Leia were already way ahead of him.

"We've got this one, Han," said Luke, as he and Leia jumped onto the extra speeder and revved it up. "Stay here and watch over the droids."

"Awwww, droid babysitting!" complained Han. "I'm not a babysitter, I'm the one who should be on that ..."

ZOOM! The speeder bike erupted, as Luke and Leia launched into the forest to chase after the biker scouts.

"... on that abandoned, super-cool speeder bike," finished Han.

Bleep, Berb, Blicka. R2-D2 stomped over to Han and zapped him lightly.

"Hey! What was that for?" he asked, hopping up and down, holding his hurt leg.

"That," C-3PO explained, "was for calling us babies."

Han sat on a fallen tree and Chewbacca moved next to him. "Well, Chewie, I guess we can't go on every adventure."

The Wookiee nodded in agreement.

Just then, a static-like buzzing came from the bushes behind them. "*Base to scouts, base to scouts, report?*" It was the biker scout's comlink!

"Chewie, I've got a great idea!" said Han, as he ran over and picked up the comlink. "If we can't go on the adventure, then let's bring the adventure to us!"

Han pressed the
button on the side
of the comlink and
said, "Uh, we had a
slight weapon
malfunction, but uh ...
everything's *not* perfectly
all right now. We're *not* fine.
We're *not at all* fine here now,
thank you. Can you send help?"

The comlink was silent for a moment
and then it buzzed again. "*We're sending out
a squad.*"

Moments later, three more biker scouts rode
through the forest on speeders, but the rebels
were ready this time. Chewie and Han knocked
the first two scouts off of their bikes, but C-3PO
missed his target and the scout zipped away.

"What happened, Threepio?" asked Han.

"He was floating and white," said C-3PO.
"I thought he was a g-g-g-ghost."

Han slapped his own head in frustration.
"OK, well, you get on Chewie's speeder. Artoo,
you're coming with me."

R2-D2 beeped and shot out a rope that
latched on to Han's speeder bike.

"Let's show Luke and Leia that we know how to have fun, too!" said Han, as they zoomed into the forest chasing after the last scout.

The wind whipped through Chewie's hair, which was sent flowing all over C-3PO. "BLECH! Will someone please help me?" C-3PO pleaded. "Now I know how a hairball feels!"

Han pulled in front with R2-D2 in tow behind him. They were catching up to the biker scout when the forest opened up into a clearing with an Imperial base. An army of stormtroopers were ready and waiting for Han's attack.

"This is one of the times I probably should have listened to the odds," Han said to himself.

He turned the speeder to fly away, but Chewie and C-3PO were right behind him. The rebels nearly crashed into each other. Poor C-3PO lost his grip and went flying into the base's giant satellite communication dish. With a tremendous crash, the dish and C-3PO came tumbling down.

"Yee-haw!" cheered Han. "Now that's what I call crashing the party, Threepio!" He swooped over and picked up the dizzy droid.

"Goodness me!" cried C-3PO. "Captain Solo, I'm sorry if I broke anything back there."

"No need to apologise, you shiny little wrecking ball," said Han. "Just hold on tight. We've got company!"

Hundreds of stormtroopers were after them. Chewie took the lead as the stormtroopers chased the rebels into the forest.

"Ha! We can lose them in the trees!" cheered Han.

"Sir, how is flying through trees at high speeds a good idea?" enquired C-3PO, but it was too late.

Han veered into the dark shadows of the trees, first left, then right, narrowly missing each towering trunk. The expert scouts veered around the same trees and crept

closer to R2-D2, who was still being pulled behind Han.

"Sir, it seems you've underestimated the scouts' driving skills," said C-3PO.

"You've got to be kidding me," said Han. "How are they missing all those trees?"

"Perhaps they are flying *through* the trees!" gasped C-3PO. "Like g-g-g-ghosts!" The droid cowered in fear and accidentally covered Han's eyes!

"I'm flying blind over here!" hollered Han. His speeder dropped closer to the forest floor,

recklessly dragging R2-D2 down into the bushes.

Whirp. Wee-Yooowww! beeped R2-D2, using his rockets

to dodge the branches. After a few near misses, R2-D2 fired a rope that stuck into a tree and snapped tightly, turning Han's speeder sharply to the left. The stormtroopers caught up with the rebels, but the scouts didn't see the rope in time. They smacked against it and were all thrown to the ground, creating a giant pile of stormtroopers.

"Whoa! Would you look at that?" said Han, as he moved C-3PO's hands out from in front of his eyes. The entire scout group had been defeated. "I told you my plan would work, Threepio."

Blerp. Bleep. Bwup. R2-D2 gave Han a second small shock.

"Hey! What was that for?" cried Han.

"Apparently this," C-3PO said, gesturing to the fallen scouts, "was all Artoo's doing."

"Oh. Uh, can you at least tell the other rebels that we beat them together as a team?" Han asked.

R2-D2 beeped and shook his head.

Before Han could say anything, they heard Chewie roar. The team rushed to the Wookiee and found Luke Skywalker with him.

"Oh my gosh, guys," said Luke. "It was SO cool riding on that speeder. At first we were all like, *nee-yow, nee-yow*, and then we were all like *shoosh, shoosh,* and there were trees and explosions, and we took down those scouts.

Trust me, they are not going to call for backup anytime soon."

"That's great, kid," said Han. "There's one little thing."

"What?" asked Luke.

"Leia," said Han.

Luke looked behind him, then all around before realising she was missing. "Oops!"

Deep in the woods, Princess Leia stood up and called for her friends. A cute little teddy bear-like creature called an Ewok found her instead. But that's a whole other story for another time ...

THE *FALCON* AWAKENS

After the battle of Endor, Han Solo and Chewbacca thought they had seen it all. Somewhere along the way, they even lost Han's prize ship, the *Millennium Falcon*.

Then years later, Han and Chewie stumbled across it again with strangers on board. Along

with a young woman named Rey, a young man named Finn and a droid named BB-8, the *Millennium Falcon* was now blasting towards the planet Takodana to reconnect with the Resistance.

"Hmmm," said Han as he wiggled back into the driver's seat. "Something feels wrong. Did you change my chair settings?"

Rey shook her head. "I don't think so."

"Good, you should never mess with a pilot's seat." Han shifted the chair back and forth, then up and down, until a mountain of sand slid out from between the cushions. "Wow, what have you been doing with my ship? Having beach parties?"

"It's been on Jakku," said Rey. "The sand gets everywhere." She opened a drawer under the dashboard and even more sand poured out, along with a beach ball. "Well, maybe someone did throw a beach party on board, but I swear it wasn't me."

"Relax, kid. I believe you," said Han, as he stood up, kicked the ball and walked towards the common room. "Remind me to have Chewie get this cleaned. He's a real wiz at making the *Falcon* look half-passable."

"I can't believe this is the actual *Millennium Falcon*!" Rey said, as she followed Han.

"The what?" asked Finn, as Rey and Han entered the lounge where he and Chewie were sitting. Finn was trying to juggle a set of remotes.

"Careful with those," said Han. "Don't let them zap my ship. I just got her back."

"This is the ship that made the Kessel Run in fourteen parsecs!" explained Rey.

"Twelve!" Han corrected her. "Not fourteen. Why do you keep getting that wrong?"

"Twelve, fourteen, what's the difference?" asked Finn, as a remote zapped him. "Ouch!"

"Don't say I didn't warn you," said Han, as Finn tried to dodge the remote's blasts.

Finally, Han grabbed the orb and shut it down. "You know these things have an off-button, right? So, what else do you think you know about me?"

Rey and Finn considered all the old stories they'd heard about Han and his legendary friends.

"Is it true," Rey started, "that Luke Skywalker saved you from freezing on Hoth?"

"Whoa, you got that backwards, kid," said Han. "Without me and one unlucky tauntaun,

Luke would have been frozen solid like a Jedi-cicle! Honestly guys, you've got me worried. You messed up my starship and now you're getting a lot of stuff wrong about me. I'll have you know that most of the time, I was the hero."

"That's not what I've heard," said Finn.

"You calling me a liar, kid?" asked Han.

"No, sir, not really," said Finn. "It's just that I grew up hearing different kinds of stories about you. There was one campfire story that

stormtroopers used to tell each other during our training ..."

"Stormtroopers?" asked Rey.

"I meant my Resistance friends," Finn said nervously. "Did I say stormtroopers? Ha, that's weird. Anyway, the stormtroo ... my friends always told me that a droid saved you and Chewie from a pack of vicious creatures known as the Ewoks."

Han paused and looked at Chewie. The Wookiee shrugged his shoulders and nodded.

"OK," admitted Han, "that one is a teeny-tiny bit true, but those Ewoks weren't vicious. They were adorable."

"So you were captured by a pack of adorable creatures?" wondered Rey.

"On second thoughts, those Ewoks were the most terrifying things in the galaxy," said Han. "They had soulless eyes and black hearts and luckily I was able to convince them to help us defeat the Empire."

"I've also heard that you only helped blow up one of the Death Stars," said Finn.

"Who told you that?" snapped Han.

"Ky- ," Finn said before catching himself. "I mean, Rylo Ken. He's just some guy, a totally normal, nice guy who doesn't wear a mask or have a lightsaber or use the Force. He told me."

"Well, this Ken guy is full of hot air," said Han. "I saved Luke from being blasted by Darth Vader, so that Luke could go on to destroy the first Death Star. I've got a medal for it here somewhere, though it's probably buried in sand now."

Sure enough, Chewie pulled the medal out of another pile of sand that was under his seat. He held it up victoriously.

Han nodded. "See? Then, along with the savage Ewoks, I shut down the shield protecting the second Death Star while my friend Lando Calrissian flew the *Millennium Falcon*. He fired the blast that blew it up."

"So you needed the adorable creatures' help to shut down the shield?" asked Rey. "And if what you're saying is true, technically you didn't blow up any Death Stars."

"Technically, I don't have to keep you on my ship right now if I don't want to," said Han. "So let's just agree that I played an important role in blowing them up."

"Good point," said Rey. "It is pretty cool that you shot down Darth Vader's starship."

"I heard Darth Vader wasn't really all that bad, anyway," said Finn. Instantly he wished he'd kept his mouth shut.

Han's eyes became super wide. "Oh, he was as bad as bad can be, kid. He froze me in carbonite so that Jabba the Hutt could use me as wall art. And if you don't want me to do the same thing to you, let's stop it with the silly questions."

Chewie let out a growl from the other side of the room.

"He's pretty big for a pet," said Finn, as he motioned to Chewbacca. "Do you have to take him out for walks?"

At that, Chewie leapt up and nearly tore through the holochess table. Han jumped between Chewie and Finn. "Take it easy, furball. Our guest doesn't

seem to understand that you're my trusted co-pilot. Or that you've ripped a droid's arms out of its sockets for saying much less."

Finn stumbled backwards and hid behind Rey.

"A word of advice," said Rey. "Leave the Wookiee alone, Finn."

Chewie grabbed the remote from Han and turned it back on. The orb flew directly behind Finn and gave him another zap. "Ouch!"

"All right, kiddos," said Han. "Here's what you need to know about me. I hate hearing the odds, I will fly into an asteroid belt if I need to in a pinch, I've been monster bait for more icky creatures than I care to remember, and I'm still here. Any other questions?"

"What does this do?" asked Finn, pointing at a giant red button labelled 'DO NOT PUSH'. As soon as he asked his question, Finn pressed the button.

Instantly, the *Millennium Falcon* stalled and fell out of hyperdrive. The move happened so

fast that all the doors opened up and the sands of Jakku came rushing in, covering Finn, Rey, Han, Chewie and BB-8.

"Kid, don't take this the wrong way, because I mean it," said Han. "Stop pressing my buttons!"

They both tried to move, but the sand had packed them in tightly.

"What now?" asked Rey.

"I've got it!" said Finn. He tossed the remote and hit another button. Before the others could say no, a vacuum started and the sand around them was cleaned up in no time.

"How did you do that?" asked Han.

"Let's just say I know a thing or two about waste management and dirty jobs," said Finn.

Han stared at Finn, then checked the map to see where they were. "Well, the good news is that we've almost arrived at our destination."

"What's the bad news?" asked Rey.

"No bad news," said Han. "I just hope you've listened and learned from my stories today."

"Sure," said Rey. "Don't mess with Chewie, Ewoks are nothing but trouble and the Empire was super evil."

"And Luke needed lots of saving, there's apparently a difference between twelve and

fourteen parsecs and you shouldn't try to juggle live remotes with blasters," added Finn.

"You forgot one thing," said Han.

"What's that?" the two travellers asked.

"I'm *always* the hero."